FINAL FEAST

THE LAST THANKSGIVING
BOOK 2

MIRA HALDEN

Copyright © 2025 by Mira Halden

All rights reserved.

No part of this book may be reproduced in any form or by any electronic or mechanical means, including information storage and retrieval systems, without written permission from the author, except for the use of brief quotations in a book review.

1984 – NEW YORK CITY

Every family has a breaking point.

For the Halems, it was not a shouted argument or a deathbed confession. It was a dinner—one that should have tethered them together, but instead left each of them quietly unmoored.

That last Thanksgiving at the house on Elm Street, sometime in the early seventies, had been the quietest implosion. Anya, the matriarch, was gone. The old rituals had been reduced to supermarket stuffing and clumsy silences. A letter had been found. A name no one recognized. And beneath all of it—a truth long buried in the ashes of another continent, in the mouths of people who had chosen silence as a form of love.

Leah had stayed behind after that meal.

Alone in the house, she discovered the first threads of a mystery that would come to define her: a box of letters, a forged identity, and the faded signature of a man called Rako Halem—her grandfather's brother. Or perhaps the man her grandfather had once been. Or both.

She had made a promise that night, to herself and to the ghosts that would not leave her: **she would uncover the truth.**

Now, more than a decade later, the house was gone. Sold quietly.

Emptied. The dining table auctioned to a stranger. The kitchen window ripped out and replaced by someone who didn't know it once grew dill.

And the family? **Scattered.**

Leah was thirty-six now.

A journalist by trade, an archivist at heart. She lived in a rent-controlled walk-up in the West Village, filled with books she hadn't yet read and folders full of leads she hadn't yet followed. The city had changed her—made her harder, quicker, fluent in the language of deadlines and deflection. But the past still clung to her ribs like a song half-remembered.

She kept the letter.

Tucked in a drawer in her desk, under a dried sprig of dill and a metro card she never used. The paper was thinner now. But its weight had only grown.

Misha had moved west. Colorado, maybe Utah. His holiday cards came with snowy mountains and single-sentence updates: *"Still breathing. Still fixing things."*

Helen lived two hours away in a cramped duplex with floral wallpaper and a ceramic angel in every room. Her children had drifted, her voice had softened, but her silences had not. Leah saw her once or twice a year. Usually out of obligation.

Sam—Helen's son—was now a social worker in Boston. His hair had gone gray early. He didn't come to family gatherings anymore, but sometimes he called Leah after midnight, voice low, asking about the old country as if it were a place they could still go.

But the center was gone.

And what remained was what always remained in the aftermath of deep legacy: fragments.

A coin.

A recipe.

A name.

A silence.

And Leah—still holding the edges, still asking questions.

It began again on a rainy Tuesday, with a message left on her office voicemail:

"Ms. Halem, this is Dr. Kovac from the Library of Eastern Diaspora Archives. You inquired years ago about the Halem family. We've come across a bundle of postwar correspondence... There's a name in there. Rako Halem. Dated 1946, Belgrade. I believe it's yours."

Leah didn't breathe.

Not fully.

Not until the line clicked off and she realized she was still holding the pen in her hand, shaking.

The past had never been buried.

It had just been waiting.

She took the letter from the drawer again that night.

The first one.

Anya's handwriting.

The name.

The confession.

She held it over a candle, briefly—not to burn it, but to watch how the paper bent, as if bracing for fire.

Then she packed a bag.

Because if the past wanted to be found again, she was ready.

The family was fractured.

But truth might still be stitched from its threads.

NEW YORK CITY, 1984 – TWO WEEKS LATER

The archives smelled of dust and disuse. The kind of silence that settled not from peace but from weight—of paper, of time, of the ghosts that clung to the margins of old ink.

Leah stood in the reading room of the Library of Eastern Diaspora Archives, third floor, under a flickering fluorescent light that buzzed like it held a grudge.

She hadn't been here in years. Not since grad school, when she'd written a paper on diaspora mourning rituals and made the mistake of crying in the middle of an oral history tape. Back then, she had still believed history could be organized. Contained. Understood.

Now she knew better.

History was a house on fire, and the archive was what survived in the attic.

Dr. Kovac was smaller than she remembered. White hair, wire glasses, the voice of someone used to being ignored until it was too late.

He handed her a folder—slim, brown, tied with string—and said only: "Handle carefully. These were sealed for decades."

Leah nodded, though her pulse had already quickened.

The folder bore no name. Only a number. A year: *1946*.

She opened it.

Inside: six pages. Handwritten. In a dialect of Serbo-Croatian that she couldn't fully read but recognized from childhood lullabies and overheard conversations in Anya's kitchen. The handwriting was slanted and fine, masculine but hesitant in places. At the top of the first page, three words in English had been stamped:

POSTWAR INTERROGATION – R. HALEM

Her breath caught.

Not "Yusuf."

Rako.

The pages weren't letters. They were **transcripts.**

She turned to the first page and began reading, slowly, haltingly, using a nearby dictionary and intuition as her guides.

The narrative emerged like a bruise beneath the skin.

Rako—or the man calling himself Rako—was being questioned by Allied forces about a printing press in Belgrade. Leaflets. Underground cells. Anti-occupation efforts. His name had surfaced in connection with a shipment of forged documents smuggled out of a partisan camp and into American hands.

There were accusations. Coded phrases. Mentions of sabotage.

And one chilling line, half-buried in the fourth page:

"We were told he changed names before. That Halem is not his first truth."

Leah sat back, heart pounding.

The "he" in question wasn't clear. It could have been Rako. Or someone else entirely. But the implication was unmistakable:

Yusuf Halem may not have just changed his name to help a cousin.

He may have taken someone else's life.

Or buried his own.

She kept reading.

By the final page, the record ended with three words stamped in heavy block type:

RELEASED. MONITORED. CLOSED.

No location. No explanation.

And no body.

Leah stared at the last page for a long time.

The archive's clock ticked above her.

Outside the windows, the sun had faded into pale gold, and the lights of the city blinked on one by one like eyes opening across the skyline.

A thousand questions rose, heavy and unformed.

Had Yusuf fled something worse than war?

Had Rako died under his name?

Had the man who raised them—who blessed bread, who called silence safety—ever truly told the truth?

Dr. Kovac returned with a photocopy of the last known address linked to the record. It was in Yugoslavia. Near the coast.

"You won't find much," he said. "The town was nearly leveled in '45. The records scattered. But the name Halem... it meant something there. Once."

Leah nodded, clutching the folder like a talisman.

That night, she opened Anya's letter again.

Ran her fingers over the words, feeling the tremble that lived beneath each sentence.

She folded it, slowly. Tucked it into her coat pocket beside the archive report.

Then, quietly, she began to plan.

She would go.

To the village.

To the ashes.

To the place where her family had first become ghosts.

Not for answers. Not entirely.

But for the voice in her blood that would not let her rest.

COASTAL BALKANS, 1984

The plane touched down in gray light, and Leah stepped onto the tarmac with a coat too thin and questions too heavy. The wind off the Adriatic smelled like salt and rust, and the sky hung low, a lid over the landscape—as if the country itself was trying to forget.

She had no map that could help her now. Only a photocopied address scrawled in the corner of a declassified intelligence file and a name that had already been worn down by time: **Halem**.

The train took her inland.

Each stop was a bleeding photograph: bomb-pocked buildings, grandmothers hunched in wool, boys chasing stray dogs through streets without names. She moved through it all like a dreamer—observing, absorbing, invisible.

By the third day, the land began to change.

Green hills rose, wild and furred with pine. The train tracks curved inland toward the town once known as **Starigrad**, though the signs had long since rusted, and even the stationmaster pronounced it differently now—his accent coarse, his eyes too tired to care.

Starigrad was not a town anymore.

It was a **memory** draped in stone and silence.

Half the buildings had collapsed into themselves—caved roofs, broken windows, bricks split by frost and fire. The old church stood like a sentinel, spire snapped clean. Smoke curled from only a handful of chimneys.

Leah disembarked with nothing but a shoulder bag and a photograph of her grandfather folded into her wallet.

She asked carefully.

Most people shook their heads.

Some refused to speak.

One woman, ancient and bent like a question mark, whispered the name **"Halem"** like it was either sacred or cursed.

"He was not from here," she said in a dialect Leah could barely follow. "But he was remembered. And not kindly."

Leah found the house by instinct.

It stood near the edge of the village, overgrown with ivy, its shutters askew like tired eyes. There was a small iron gate, nearly devoured by weeds. Someone had carved a symbol into the stone beside the doorframe—a mark she did not recognize, but which made her shiver.

She knocked.

Once.

Twice.

Nothing.

She turned to leave—then heard a voice, hoarse and clipped, from within.

"You're late."

The door opened slowly.

A man stood inside, cane in hand, face like carved oak—lined and weather-worn, with dark eyes that saw too much.

He looked at her the way one looks at a shadow that moves wrong.

"I thought you were done looking," he said in English, heavily accented but sharp. "But I see the girl kept digging."

Leah froze.

"You know who I am?"

"I knew your grandfather."

"Yusuf?"

A silence stretched between them like a held breath.

Then: "No. **Rako**."

His name was **Marko Halem**.

He was not her uncle. Or cousin. Or anything simple.

He was **what remained**—a branch too thin to bear the family tree, but rooted in the same earth. His father had been Rako's brother. Or Yusuf's. Or perhaps both. The story bent each time it was told.

"You look like her," Marko said, gesturing to a dusty table where a yellowed photograph sat beneath cracked glass. Anya, young. Holding a child. Her eyes bright with hope and something else—**warning**.

"I came for the truth," Leah said.

Marko laughed—a dry, papery sound. "You think we have truth left here? Truth burns like bread in war."

"I need to know who Yusuf was. Or Rako. Or whoever he was before America."

Marko's smile faded. His hands trembled slightly as he poured dark tea into a chipped cup.

"There was a time he was both. And a time he was neither."

That night, by the fire, Marko told her pieces.

Not the whole story—never that. But fragments.

"Rako was clever. Too clever. The kind of man who made enemies without realizing it... or maybe realizing it too well."

"He forged papers. But not for freedom. For escape. From a choice he didn't make, and one he did."

"There were leaflets. A betrayal. A body burned in his place. And then, suddenly—he was gone. Gone to your country. Wearing the name Halem like a mask."

Leah took notes in the dim light, heart thudding with every half-revealed truth.

"Did he kill anyone?"

Marko didn't answer.

But he didn't deny it either.

Before bed, she asked to see what was left.

Marko led her to a trunk buried in dust and moths.

Inside:

- A child's sweater, hand-stitched.
- A rosary, burned at one end.
- A tin case filled with old ration coupons.
- And at the very bottom: **a passport.**

She pulled it out with shaking hands.

It was stamped 1937.

The photo inside was unmistakable—**Yusuf**, but younger. Labeled not as Yusuf.

Not even as Rako.

But as a third name.

"Niko Juric."

Leah sat on the cold floor, stunned.

The story was not linear.

It was a spiral.

A circle of names, layered over one another like soot.

And she had only just begun to uncover the core.

She looked up at Marko.

"Why would he change it so many times?"

Marko lit a cigarette and stared into the fire.

"When you run long enough," he said, "you forget which name was yours first. Only the lie survives."

Outside, the wind howled.

And far off, beyond the crumbling walls of Starigrad, snow began to fall—quiet and heavy.

The world covering itself once again.
But Leah would not forget.
She had a name now.
She had **three**.
And she had a question that would not leave her bones:
Whose life had her grandfather lived?

STARIGRAD, BALKANS – WINTER, 1984

The truth came quietly.

Not as a shout, but as a sigh.

Not in a file or a confession, but in the slow breath of an old man who had held it too long.

Marko's health waned over the following days. A cough settled into his lungs like an occupying army, and the cold reached deeper into the bones of the house. Still, he refused to leave. He had lived too long in these walls to die anywhere else.

Leah stayed.

She brought him broth and helped chop wood for the stove, her city hands blistering against the ax handle. In the evenings, she read aloud from old books in fractured translation—stories about borders and faith and names that meant different things in different mouths.

On the fifth day, when the cough had quieted to a rattle, Marko told her everything.

"There were two brothers," he said.

Leah sat at the foot of the bed, notebook forgotten in her lap.

"Yusuf and Rako?"

Marko shook his head slowly. "That's where you're wrong. That was never the truth. That was the lie they agreed on."

He reached beneath his pillow and pulled out a creased photograph.

Two boys, standing in front of a stone house. One was taller, sterner, with sharp eyes. The other—slighter, with a crooked smile.

"Which is Yusuf?" Leah whispered.

Marko tapped the smiling boy.

"He was born **Rako Halem**. And he was the one who died."

Leah went still. Her breath caught, her vision thinned.

"I don't understand," she said, even though she did.

"Rako was a rebel. Not with a gun—he didn't have the stomach. But with words. He printed leaflets. Fed information. Wrote poems that mocked the fascists. That sort of thing could get you killed. It almost did."

Marko's voice broke.

"There was a raid. A night of fire and dogs. They came for Rako. But it was **Yusuf**—his quiet, careful brother—who was there. And Rako... he ran."

Marko closed his eyes.

"They found the body days later. Burned. Dressed in Rako's coat. Carrying his satchel. Everyone believed it was Rako who died. And Yusuf who lived."

"But it wasn't," Leah said.

"No," Marko whispered. "It was the other way around. **Rako survived. Yusuf burned.**"

Leah felt dizzy.

"So he took his brother's name?"

"He had to. The fascists still wanted Rako dead. So he crossed the sea with Yusuf's papers. Became him. Married under his name. Buried the past so deep, it stopped breathing."

She tried to stand, but the room tilted. Her knees locked.

Everything unraveled.

The man she'd called grandfather—his quiet, his distance, his hesitations around his own story—it made sense now. He hadn't just been hiding *from* something. He had been hiding *as* someone.

Her real grandfather had died in a fire.

His name was Yusuf.

And the man she'd loved—Anya's husband, the father of her family—had lived inside the name like a borrowed coat.

"There was more," Marko added softly. "Things he never told. A woman, maybe. Before Anya. Maybe even a child."

Leah's head snapped up.

"You're saying—"

"I'm saying he was not the man you thought. But he tried. He tried to be better than what was left of him."

That night, Leah sat alone beside the fire, the photo of the two boys clutched in her hand.

A name is supposed to be a promise. A tether. A lineage.

But for her family, names had been currency. Armor. Disguise.

Rako Halem had become **Yusuf Halem.**

And with that choice, everything had shifted.

A war.

A marriage.

A child.

A legacy.

All of it forged in the crucible of survival.

She thought of Anya—how fiercely she had guarded the quiet. How gently she had protected a man who was never quite hers, and yet entirely so.

Leah wept. Not from betrayal, but from the immensity of it all.

How far a soul must run to feel safe in another name.

The next morning, Marko was gone.

She found him in his sleep, face turned toward the window, as if waiting for snow.

On the table beside him, a single sheet of paper. A map. Drawn in shaking pencil. A town on the border. A name circled.
"Petra Juric."
The last thread.

Leah folded the photo, the letter, the map—all of it—into her bag.
The journey wasn't over.
There was a woman.
There was a child.
And there was still a truth buried somewhere beyond the edge of war and family, waiting to be unearthed.
As she boarded the bus to the border, she whispered the names to herself—not to remember them, but to set them free.
Rako. Yusuf. Juric. Halem.
Each a wound.
Each a key.

NEW YORK, WINTER 1984

The message came folded on her hotel pillow, slid under the door by a boy too young to know he'd delivered a fracture.

"Your mother is in the hospital. Call immediately."

There was no punctuation, no warmth. Just impact.

Leah read it twice before she moved. Her hand trembled as she reached for the rotary phone beside the nightstand. She hadn't spoken to Helen in months—words had become slippery between them, brittle and barbed. The last thing they'd said to each other was not an apology, but an avoidance.

Now it echoed.

The voice on the line belonged to a nurse who sounded too tired to offer comfort.

"Minor stroke. She was found early. Stable, for now. She's asking for you."

The world narrowed.

Leah flew back across the ocean with the map of Rako Halem still folded in her coat pocket, the names she had unearthed still pulsing at her fingertips. But they felt suddenly weightless—like heirlooms she didn't have permission to touch anymore.

At the hospital, the smell of antiseptic and metal swallowed her whole.

Helen lay in a narrow bed near the window, her skin a shade too pale and her left hand curled in on itself like a question that would never fully be answered. Machines hummed beside her, impersonating stability.

Her hair had thinned. Her face had softened. She looked older than her mother had, in those last days.

"Mom," Leah whispered.

Helen opened one eye.

And for a terrible second, she didn't speak.

Then, hoarsely: "You came back."

Leah nodded. "Of course."

Helen's mouth twitched, not quite a smile. "I always thought you'd miss my funeral. Too busy... chasing ghosts."

It was a joke. Barely.

But it landed like a stone.

They sat in silence for a while. The kind of silence that meant everything had already been said—and nothing had been resolved.

Eventually, Helen spoke again. Slower now.

"Your grandfather... he was a good man. Quiet. Careful. That was enough, back then."

Leah hesitated.

She had so many truths to offer. Pages of them. Names. Documents. A story burned clean through with sorrow.

But when she looked at Helen—hooked to wires, her voice thinner than breath—she couldn't give it to her. Not like this.

"There's more to him than we knew," Leah said carefully.

Helen's eyes flicked toward her.

"There always was. That's what made him so hard to love. And so easy to forgive."

That night, Leah stayed in the waiting room. She didn't sleep.

Instead, she took out the photograph of Rako and Yusuf—boys before the world broke them.

She held it beneath the light and studied their faces.

They could have been twins.

But only one had made it to America. Only one had survived—and survival had made him someone else.

Helen's monitors beeped steadily in the next room, reminding Leah with every tick: **the past may wait, but the living do not.**

By morning, Helen was resting more easily.

The doctor said recovery would be slow, but likely.

Still, something in Leah had shifted.

Time was no longer something to investigate—it was something to salvage.

If there were bridges left to rebuild, she had to start now.

Before history became eulogy.

As she stepped into the hospital hallway, Leah pulled out her notebook.

And in the margin of the last page, she wrote three words:

"Final Thanksgiving. Soon."

She didn't yet know what it would look like.

Who would come.

Or what it would cost to gather them all again.

But it was the only thing that made sense now.

A reckoning.

A table.

A return.

ELM STREET, NEW JERSEY – AUTUMN, 2005

The letter came not from a lawyer, but a cousin—one of those second-removed, never-quite-close ones with a firm handshake and no patience for sentiment.

"Thought you should know," it read. "We're selling the house. It's time."

No flourish. No question. Just **finality**.

Leah read it three times before setting it on the table beside her untouched coffee. The words hung in the morning air like smoke.

The house.

Their house.

Not just hers. Not just Helen's. But a layered archive of breath and silence and dinners no one remembered clearly but still carried inside them like a scent.

The house where Anya once sang to seeds on a windowsill.

Where Yusuf—Rako—sat at the head of a table he never fully believed he belonged to.

Where Helen had stormed out, and later returned, smaller somehow.

Where Leah had first learned the shape of grief by watching her family lose each other one quiet act at a time.

It had been shuttered for years. Untouched. A hushed museum of old chairs and inherited dust.

Now it would belong to someone else.

She drove out the next morning.

The keys came in a manila envelope with no note. Just a label in fading ink: "**Halem.**"

She paused at the curb.

The lawn was overgrown. The shutters hung crookedly, and the walkway had cracked in a dozen places. The porch still creaked, like a voice trying to remember its line.

But the bones of it were intact.

Leah stepped inside.

And it was like walking into breath held too long.

The air was stale with memory. The walls still bore faint outlines of old frames—children, graduations, faces lost to time.

The kitchen smelled faintly of wood polish and silence.

She touched the table. Still there. Scarred from decades of elbows and dropped knives and prayer. She imagined Anya at the stove. Yusuf bent over bills. Helen as a girl, defiant. Herself as a child, watching.

The rooms echoed.

This was where their Thanksgivings had lived—and died.

And maybe, she thought, **it was where they had to be reborn.**

The idea struck her not like lightning, but like dawn: slow, inevitable, impossible to ignore.

One more Thanksgiving.

A final one.

Not for celebration. Not for nostalgia.

But for reckoning.

For naming the truths that had been folded away in drawers, tucked into photo albums, buried under a century of silence.

The house would be sold. But not yet.

Not before the story was finished.

She spent the night in her old bedroom.

The wallpaper had yellowed. The closet still held a scarf her mother once wore.

Outside, wind scraped dry leaves across the windows like someone whispering secrets in the dark.

Leah sat at the desk and began to write.

Not a history. Not yet.

Invitations.

Not to a meal, but to a confrontation.

To a last attempt at wholeness.

Would they come?

The cousins from Queens who'd stopped speaking to Helen after the funeral?

Helen's sister-in-law, who claimed Leah had "stirred things up" with her questions?

The grandson of Kerem—now a quiet teacher in Chicago, barely connected by blood but part of the same haunted root system?

She didn't know.

But she would try.

Because the house deserved one more story.

And the family needed a table, even if it cracked beneath the weight of what they had left unsaid.

In the morning, she stood in the doorway and whispered, "One more Thanksgiving."

The house creaked in reply.

LATE AUTUMN, 2005 – ACROSS STATES AND SILENCES

The idea of writing them all at once overwhelmed her.

So Leah wrote one invitation a night, as if summoning a ghost each time. Not the glossy kind that came in holiday envelopes—no embossed acorns, no warm platitudes. Just plain white paper, her own uneven handwriting, and the starkness of the ask.

"**One last Thanksgiving. At the house. If you can come, please do.**"

Each name brought its own knot of feeling. Each envelope felt heavier than paper should.

She sealed them slowly, deliberately, like she was closing something behind her.

To Helen, she delivered it in person, despite the coolness that had hung between them since the hospital. They sat on the porch together, bundled in mismatched sweaters, a quiet too long to call peaceful settling between them.

Helen read the note aloud, voice flat. "One last Thanksgiving?"

Leah nodded. "At the house. Before it's gone."

Helen exhaled. "You're always looking backward."

"I'm not," Leah said, too quickly. "I'm trying to bring everyone forward. One more time. One more story."

Her mother's gaze stayed on the street. "If it's one more story, you better hope they're ready to hear it."

To cousin Miriam, she mailed a second copy after the first came back unopened. This time, she included a dried dill sprig tucked inside a napkin from Anya's linen drawer—old, but still soft.

She never received a reply.

To Avi, she added a photograph of the long dining table at the Elm Street house—empty, sunlit, waiting.

He called three days later.

"I don't have time to dig up all that history, Leah. What's the point? We survived. That should be enough."

"It's not," she said. "Survival isn't the end of the story."

He hung up without another word.

But two days later, he emailed a flight confirmation.

To Jacob, she almost didn't write at all.

He'd been angry since the funeral. Since Leah had brought up Yusuf's dual identity, the possibility of a brother buried beneath his name. He said it was "disrespectful" to excavate a man who had worked so hard to forget.

But in the end, she sent it anyway.

His reply came by postcard, in cramped handwriting:

"Fine. I'll come. But don't ask me to talk about the past. Some things deserve silence."

To Rosa's granddaughter, Leah wrote with hesitation. They'd never met. She barely knew her name—Elena. But the stories from the tenement echoed too loud to ignore.

Elena's response was a voicemail, her voice shaking slightly.

"My grandmother used to say your family had thunder in its blood. I never knew what she meant until I heard my mother cry over someone named Yusuf last year. I'll be there. Even if I don't know why."

Some answers came with resentment.

One cousin accused her of "turning grief into a spectacle."

Another asked if the food would be kosher, vegan, or whatever the latest "family standard" was.

Someone sent back the envelope, torn in half.

Still, others arrived like quiet confessions:

"I think I need this."

"I haven't been home in thirty years."

"Do you still have Anya's bread recipe?"

And then there was the letter to **Petra**.

It felt like writing to a myth. A name on a map. A woman who might have once loved Rako—or Yusuf—or both.

Leah's letter was careful. Gentle. Honest.

"You were part of his life. I've found your name in old documents. I believe you knew my grandfather before he became who he was to us. I don't know if you'll come. But if you do, I'll be there. Ready to listen."

She added a return address.

She didn't expect an answer.

By the end of the month, her fridge was covered in taped responses—emails, scribbled notes, postcards folded in half.

A mosaic of grief and suspicion.

Of nostalgia, guilt, and reluctant hope.

Not everyone said yes.

But enough did.

Enough to make the house feel like a heartbeat again.

She stood in the center of the kitchen on a rainy Thursday and whispered aloud:

"They're coming."

Not all of them.
Not joyfully.
But they were coming.
And that, somehow, felt holy.

ELM STREET – TWO WEEKS BEFORE THANKSGIVING, 2005

The house exhaled when she opened the kitchen windows.
Like it had been holding its breath for decades.
Cold wind swept in through the torn screens, stirring curtains stiff with age. Outside, the trees on Elm Street dropped the last of their leaves in quiet resignation. Inside, Leah stood barefoot on the cracked linoleum, sleeves rolled to her elbows, flour on her cheekbone like a fingerprint from the past.
She turned on the faucet. The pipes groaned in protest. The water came, rust-tinged and slow.
Still, it would do.

The table had been scrubbed down to the woodgrain. The yellowed lace runner—Anya's, still stained in the corner from beets or wine or some long-forgotten spill—was laid flat beneath a bowl of apples. Not decorative apples. Real ones. Bruised, uneven. Chosen because they looked like the kind Anya would've bartered for in 1915.
Leah had brought the recipes with her, though none were ever written. They lived in her margins—in scribbled memories, oral footnotes, half-told stories that began with "I remember Anya once used..." and ended with a shrug.

There were no measurements. No times or temperatures. Only instinct. Only memory.

And so she began to cook.

Not to impress. Not to nourish.

But to conjure.

First: the bread.

Beet-streaked, faintly sweet, touched with dill from sprigs she grew in a mason jar by her Brooklyn window. She kneaded the dough the way her grandmother had—forceful, rhythmic, muttering under her breath like it was a prayer.

And as her hands worked the flour and memory into form, **the house flickered—**

—Anya, 1914, leaning over the table, palms red from beets, Yusuf beside her, eyes hollow from work, but watching her as if the bread might carry them across a continent of grief.

"We eat," Anya had said then, "because we are still here."

Then: the potatoes. Mashed with browned butter and browned onions, folded with a splash of vinegar—an oddity she remembered Helen calling "peasant fancy."

As she stirred, Leah saw Helen at sixteen—chopping onions angrily after a fight with her father, muttering curses in both English and the language she never taught Leah. The kitchen had smelled like salt and defiance.

Next: the chicken. Not turkey. Not this year.

Anya had roasted chicken with garlic and herbs and a honey glaze she had learned from a neighbor from Minsk. It was sticky, aromatic, deeply golden.

Leah brushed the glaze across the bird slowly, thinking of Yusuf's hands carving meat with the precision of someone who never expected abundance.

She brewed tea, too—chamomile, lemon rind, a pinch of sugar stolen from old habit.

In 1945, Anya had brewed the same for Helen after the war ended, when letters stopped arriving, and Yusuf refused to speak of the son they'd buried with silence. It was tea that made them sit at the table again. Not to heal. Just to sit.

And finally, **the soup.**

Cabbage, onion, scraps of bone for broth. Humble. Honest.

Leah stirred it slowly, and the steam rose like incense.

The house began to fill—not with people, not yet—but with **scent**.

The scent of arrival.

Of memory.

Of all the years between a tenement stove and a modern oven.

Of ghosts made edible.

That night, Leah sat alone at the table and tasted everything. She closed her eyes with each bite, letting it carry her backward, letting it stitch something torn.

She didn't cry.

She just ate.

And whispered aloud to the walls:

"They're coming."

The soup simmered in reply.

ELM STREET – THANKSGIVING DAY, 2005

They arrived like weather.

Some early, full of forced cheer and casseroles in foil. Some late, trailing silence and suspicion. Some didn't come at all—but their absences filled chairs just the same.

Leah stood at the window when the first car pulled up. A cousin from Chicago, stiff in a tie he kept loosening. Then Rosa's granddaughter—Elena—with a small paper-wrapped gift and wary eyes. Then Avi, alone, carrying nothing but his coat and a storm of skepticism.

Helen came last, driven by a neighbor. She wore her pearls but hadn't brushed her hair.

No one hugged.

Not at first.

The greetings were half-hearted, held back by time, pride, and the slow erosion of shared memory.

The kitchen filled with bodies. Voices overlapped. Names were forgotten. Someone asked where the good dishes were. Someone else asked where the bathroom had moved to, as if the house itself had changed in their absence.

No one asked why the lights flickered in the hallway.

No one mentioned the chair that had been removed from the table.

Leah stood in the doorway of the kitchen, watching it all like a conductor preparing for a dissonant symphony.

The meal began in awkward shuffles.

Plates passed the wrong way. Forks clinked too loudly. Elena offered a prayer in her grandmother's dialect—no one joined, but no one interrupted. It hung in the air like steam.

Helen didn't touch the bread.

Avi picked at the chicken, then finally muttered, "It's sweet. Why is it sweet?"

"It's how Anya made it," Leah said quietly.

"I remember it different."

"You were five," someone muttered.

A brief silence followed.

Then someone laughed.

Short. Bitter. Tired.

By the second course, the wine had begun to loosen things. Tongues and tempers both.

"So what's the real reason we're here?" asked Jacob, his tie already undone.

Leah folded her napkin. "To eat. To remember."

"Remember what?" he said. "Guilt? The letters? The man who lied to half of us for half a century?"

Helen flinched. "Don't."

"No, really," Jacob went on. "You dig up Yusuf's secrets, stir the pot, then serve us a meal like it'll cleanse us? You think food fixes this?"

"I think it's a start," Leah said, voice even.

Avi leaned back. "You found something, didn't you?"

She didn't answer at first.

Then, slowly, she rose.

From the sideboard, she pulled the envelope.

The **letter**.

Anya's. Addressed not to any of them, but to a name still soft on Leah's tongue.

She held it like a match, trembling.

"This was hidden in Anya's sewing box. It's part of what sent me digging."

Jacob groaned. "Not this again."

But others leaned in.

Leah unfolded the paper with care.

"*To R.*," she read aloud. "*I never asked you why you changed your name. I knew there was more than one truth in you. And I loved you anyway.*"

The room was silent.

The furnace kicked on.

Somewhere outside, wind knocked gently at the windows.

Helen reached for her glass, hands shaking.

"He burned his letters," she whispered. "In the hospital. I saw him."

Leah nodded. "Because he didn't want us to know who he was before America."

"Who was he?" Elena asked, gently.

Leah looked at them—her family, fractured, freckled with stubbornness and half-mended history.

"I think he was someone else's brother," she said. "And maybe someone else's husband. I think he changed his name to escape something. Or to save someone."

A long breath passed through the table like a prayer.

"And I think he loved us. Even in hiding."

No one spoke for a long while.

Then, quietly, Avi said, "I used to think Thanksgiving was invented to lie to ourselves about what we took and what we lost."

"It was," Jacob muttered.

"But maybe," Avi went on, "it's also about trying again. Even if the story's cracked."

Helen raised her glass.

"To cracked stories."

They all drank.

Even Jacob.

Even Leah.

Later, after the table was cleared, Leah found herself alone in the kitchen, hands in soapy water, sleeves rolled up like Anya's once were.

She looked around.

The stove. The window. The empty chair.

The echoes were softer now.

But still there.

And in the living room, through a thin wall, someone began to tell a story.

Not a perfect one.

But a true one.

And others listened.

ELM STREET – NIGHT OF THANKSGIVING, 2005

The dishes were washed. The wine bottles drained. The warmth in the house was artificial—dry heat from old vents, layered with the lingering scent of roasted garlic and cloves. But something else hummed beneath it, too. Not heat. Not noise.

Memory.

The kind that settles between floorboards and behind closed cabinet doors.

Leah moved through the house like a caretaker of silence. She picked up crumpled napkins, refolded them without purpose. Someone had left their scarf on the banister. The hallway light flickered when she passed beneath it.

In the dining room, the long table remained mostly intact. Plates stacked, glasses fogged, a smear of cranberry like a wound across the edge of the linen.

But at the far end—farthest from the kitchen, nearest the window—**a single chair remained untouched.**

It was intentional.

Set quietly that morning before anyone arrived. No plate. No fork. Just a white linen napkin folded like a prayer on the seat.

Some had asked.

Most hadn't.

But they noticed.

Because absence, when placed deliberately in a room, becomes louder than any voice.

Jacob had seen it first, brow furrowing. "Someone else coming?"

Leah didn't answer then. She just adjusted the napkin.

Avi glanced at it during dessert, but said nothing—only refilled his wine.

Even Helen's eyes had lingered there, softening for a brief moment before looking away.

Now, long after they'd all moved to the living room—where cousins were piecing together names of ancestors from Leah's notebook, where Elena sat on the carpet flipping through Anya's old folktale book—Leah stood in the doorway to the dining room, facing that chair.

She stepped toward it.

Kneeling, she smoothed the cloth. Adjusted the legs to be square with the table.

And then, beneath her breath, she spoke.

Not to the room.

Not to the people still in it.

But to **them**.

The ones who had no graves they could visit.

The ones whose names were altered, erased, or never known.

The ones who left and never returned.

And the ones Yusuf had buried in silence so deep it had become inheritance.

"Here is your place," she whispered. "We remember."

Behind her, someone entered quietly.

It was Helen. Her steps slow. Careful.

She stared at the chair.

After a long moment, she asked, "Was this for him?"

Leah nodded.

"Him. And whoever else never got a seat."

Helen blinked hard, her voice trembling. "I still see him sometimes. Yusuf. Standing by the stove. Watching us."

"I do too," Leah said. "Especially now."

Helen sat down in the chair beside the empty one.

"I never knew what to say to him at the end," she said. "I was still angry."

Leah looked at her mother. "He probably was too."

Helen let out a brittle laugh. "Then I suppose we were even."

More footsteps.

Avi appeared in the doorway, his mouth still stained from wine, his eyes glassy with something unsaid.

"I was thinking," he began slowly, "about the idea of a minyan. The ten you need to say Kaddish properly."

"We're not ten," Helen said.

Avi glanced toward the living room, where Elena and Jacob were still talking.

"Maybe we are," he said. "Or close enough."

He stepped past them, walked to the head of the table, and stood behind the empty chair.

"I'd like to say something," he said. "For all of them. For all of us."

Leah felt the breath catch in her chest.

She nodded.

And Avi, whose Hebrew had rusted from decades of disuse, cleared his throat and began—

"*Yitgadal v'yitkadash shmei raba...*"

His voice cracked.

But he kept going.

And one by one, they rose.

Not all knowing the words.

Not all knowing why.

But they rose.

For the missing chair.
For the man they misunderstood.
For the woman who remembered in flour and lullabies.
For the children who grew up between languages.
For the truth that had cost them more than they'd ever admitted.

They said nothing when the prayer ended.
Just stood there.
Together.
Not whole.
But somehow—less broken.

ELM STREET – THANKSGIVING NIGHT, 2005

The house didn't sleep, not really.

It rested, yes—but like a sentry, one eye always open. The walls listened. The pipes stirred. The windows sighed.

The meal had been cleared but not forgotten. Dishes stacked like uneasy treaties. The air still smelled faintly of rosemary and roasted chicken, mingled with dust, time, and a kind of ancestral exhaustion.

In the living room, the cousins sat in a sprawl of legs and paper plates, their voices quieter now, as if even laughter felt sacred in this house. The youngest ones passed old photographs back and forth like relics from an unfamiliar religion. They held them carefully, reverently, and without quite understanding the gods they belonged to.

Helen sat in her father's armchair—not as a queen but as a witness, wrapped in a shawl that had once belonged to Anya. Her eyes were red, but dry now, rimmed with the kind of tired that comes from resisting the weight of inheritance. A stack of folded linens sat untouched beside her. Leah had placed them there earlier without explanation. She had not dared to ask if Helen remembered how to fold them the "old way."

And then, **Uncle Saul rose.**

No one noticed at first—not until the chair made that groaning sound against the hardwood. Not until the room instinctively stilled.

He had sat silent for most of the day. His hands had trembled over his utensils, his posture coiled like an old book left half-read. A war veteran. A widower. The last living link to the stories no one had dared commit to paper.

He rose slowly, like a man testing the strength of his memory.

In his hand was a plain glass—thick-rimmed, with a small crack spidering near the base. Red wine sloshed inside, not yet drunk. He held it like a relic. Or maybe like a torch.

Then he cleared his throat and said, quietly, almost to himself:

"Zei gezunt."

Be well.

A hush fell over the table like a curtain being drawn.

It wasn't the words. It was the sound.

The **language.**

Yiddish. Not the peppered, joke-shop kind. Not the words that survived only in kvetching and crosswords. But whole. Full. Unbroken.

A tongue they hadn't heard spoken with sincerity since... when?

Since Anya sang lullabies?

Since Yusuf muttered prayers by the stove?

Since Saul himself was a boy, whispering translations in synagogue corners, ashamed of being between two worlds?

Now it returned—not proudly. Not theatrically. But as if it had been sleeping in his chest all this time, waiting for the room to finally be quiet enough.

He went on:

"Far di vos zenen nit mit undz haynt."

For those who are not with us tonight.

His voice didn't crack. But something else did.

Something **in** the room.

Elena set her wine down carefully. Leah went still, hand frozen mid-air above a plate of sliced apples. Avi looked away, jaw clenched.

Even Helen—the fiercest among them—closed her eyes.

Saul inhaled. Deep. Ragged.

Then he lifted his glass a little higher.

"Tsu di ershte tog, un tsu di letste."

To the first day, and to the last.

And finally—he turned to Leah.

His voice dropped lower. Intimate. Thick with memory.

"Daynu."

It would have been enough.

It wasn't the word alone. It was the tone. The *history* inside it.

The implication that everything they'd survived—the loss, the crossings, the broken dinners, the letters burned in silence, the lies told for love—should have been too much.

And yet... they had arrived here. In this house. At this table.

And for one flickering moment, they were together.

That, in itself, was a kind of miracle.

The room didn't erupt into applause. No clapping. No laughter.

Just silence.

The kind of silence that blooms after a confession, or a birth.

Leah stepped forward.

She had no old tongue. Her Yiddish was spotty—threadbare from disuse. She had learned it not from Saul or Helen, but from bedtime murmurs, from the margin notes in Anya's folktale book, from half-sung lullabies with words her mother never translated.

But something rose in her now—not language, but rhythm. An echo. A pulse.

She lifted her glass.

"My grandmother once said," she began, "that Thanksgiving was never about the pilgrims. Not for us."

She looked around the table. No one interrupted.

"For us, it was about staying. About sitting down at the table again, even when you didn't want to. Even when your hands were empty."

She swallowed. Her voice wavered.

"Even when you couldn't say who you really were."

And then, gently, she said:

"May we all be remembered in the language we forgot."

They drank.

Not to tradition. Not to nation.

But to **endurance**.

To bread that tasted like memory. To names that had been changed. To the ghosts who arrived anyway. To stories that hurt but healed. To family as an act of will, not just blood.

They drank for Anya.

They drank for Yusuf.

And somewhere, just outside the window, snow began to fall.

Soft. Silent. Enough.

ELM STREET – LATE THANKSGIVING NIGHT, 2005

The storm had slowed.

Snow clung to the windowpanes in soft, uneven drifts, the kind that made the world feel hushed, as if time itself had paused to listen.

The house was dim now. Dishes dried on a towel by the sink. A single candle still burned on the table, its flame swaying gently, casting shadows that moved like memory across the walls. In the living room, a few cousins had dozed off. Leah had pulled an old quilt from the hall closet and laid it across Jacob and Elena without waking them. Avi sat near the bookshelf, flipping through an album with slow, reverent fingers.

The house had absorbed the day—the arguments, the tears, the prayers spoken in nearly forgotten tongues—and now it waited. As if something more still needed to happen.

At 11:17 p.m., **the doorbell rang.**

It wasn't a friendly sound.

Not like bells in holiday films or memory. It buzzed harshly, twice, then fell silent.

Leah stood from the couch, heart already hammering. Who rings a bell at this hour? In this storm?

Helen stirred in the armchair but said nothing. Her eyes were open, watchful. Wide.

Leah moved to the door and opened it.

Standing on the porch, haloed in snow and moonlight, was a stranger.

He wore a wool coat and a scarf wound tight around his neck. A travel-worn satchel was slung across one shoulder, damp from the weather. He held a folded umbrella in one gloved hand. In the other, a **letter**.

He was no more than fifty. Maybe younger. But something in his face carried an older grief—one passed down, not lived. His eyes were Yusuf's eyes.

Leah blinked. "Can I help you?"

He removed his glove and spoke in quiet, accented English.

"I am called Lev."

He paused, snow collecting on his shoulders.

"I am... your cousin."

The room did not breathe when he entered.

Helen sat upright. Avi leaned forward, eyes narrowing. Jacob stirred and sat up from the couch.

Lev stood just inside the doorway, awkward but composed. He looked around slowly—at the yellowed wallpaper, the framed photograph of Anya and Yusuf near the stairs, the coat hooks by the door where a child's wool hat still hung.

"This house," he said, almost to himself. "It looks like the one I imagined."

He removed the satchel and opened it. Inside, wrapped in a cloth, were **photographs**—sepia and black-and-white, curled at the edges. He placed them on the table with trembling care.

One by one, Leah picked them up.

A boy, maybe ten, standing beside a younger Yusuf, both grinning, holding a fishing net in a field near what might have been the Dniester River.

A letter, yellowed with time, written in Yusuf's handwriting. In Yiddish.

A newspaper clipping, dated 1939. A man arrested for distributing banned pamphlets—his face obscured, but his name was listed as *Kerem Halem*.

And finally, **a forged birth certificate.**

But this one wasn't for Yusuf.

It was for *Joseph Halem*. Yusuf's paper "brother." His other self.

Lev's voice shook now.

"My grandfather was Kerem," he said. "He came to Marseille. Then to Venezuela. Then... nowhere. He died young. But he always said there was someone in America who gave him a name. A life."

Helen stood slowly, as if her legs could barely carry the weight of what she was hearing.

Leah looked up from the letter. "He wasn't Yusuf's brother."

"No," Lev said. "But he became one."

He touched the photograph gently.

"Yusuf saved his life. And changed his own. My mother—we always knew there was something hidden. But no one knew this."

Helen stepped closer. Her voice was thin. Disbelieving.

"Why come now?"

Lev looked up at her with quiet apology.

"Because the stories are dying faster than the people. And I didn't want this one to vanish, too."

He pulled one final thing from his coat pocket—a thin, worn envelope.

"This," he said, "was addressed to Anya. It was never sent."

Leah opened it with care.

Inside was a letter. It was brief. No date. But it was unmistakably Yusuf's handwriting.

My name was never mine.

But it is now hers. And she made it real.

If I am remembered, let it be for love. Not truth.

No one spoke.

Not even the walls.

And yet, everything seemed to echo.

Leah closed her eyes and felt it ripple through her—the truth, yes. But more than that: the forgiveness.

Yusuf had carried more than the weight of survival. He had borne the cost of someone else's life on his back like a secret child. He had stitched lies into love. And now, finally, the stitches had come undone.

Lev stood in the silence and said, softly:

"I did not come to break anything. Only to return a thread."

And then, from the corner of the room, Helen said—barely audible:

"Stay."

Lev looked up.

She cleared her throat, tears now openly falling. "Tomorrow... we'll eat the rest. We'll tell you everything we know. You should be part of it."

Leah placed a hand on the empty chair still waiting by the window.

"For him," she said. "For you. For everyone who came under the wrong name but still arrived."

Lev nodded.

And for the first time, **he wept.**

ELM STREET – THE DAY AFTER THANKSGIVING, 2005

The snow had not melted. It had simply settled—heavier now, and quieter.

The neighborhood lay still, muffled by drifts and the hush that only comes after something holy or painful has passed. Inside the old house on Elm Street, morning unfurled slowly. The air smelled of warmth—onions, rosemary, the faint citrusy sharpness of vinegar and boiled beets.

Leah stood barefoot in the kitchen, apron already dusted in flour, a tea towel over her shoulder like a badge. She stirred, chopped, ladled. She had been cooking since dawn. Not because she had to. But because something inside her needed to keep the flame going.

The family hadn't left. After Lev arrived with the letters, the photographs, and the name that cracked the myth of Yusuf wide open, no one had said it aloud—but **they stayed**.

They stayed because something old had been disturbed, and something older had been returned.

They stayed because no one could quite leave without finishing what had begun.

By noon, Helen was helping in the kitchen.

She didn't say much. But she peeled carrots and mashed potatoes with the quiet efficiency of someone remembering muscle memory from long ago. Every once in a while, she would hum. Not songs, but fragments—half-tunes from Anya's lullabies, melodies carried down not by sound but by scent, by texture, by repetition.

When Leah took out the jar of preserved lemon slices Anya had once used to brighten winter stews, Helen stopped.

"You remembered that?"

Leah nodded.

Helen swallowed. "I forgot I had."

They set the table together.

This time, there were no place cards. No fixed seats. No hierarchy.

Only **plates, glasses, bread.**

And three empty chairs.

Not explained. Not defended.

But present.

They gathered slowly.

Jacob was first, rubbing the back of his neck like a man coming into court. He nodded at Helen. Said nothing. Sat down.

Avi followed, shoulders still stiff with the pride that had always kept him from crying at funerals or hugging without awkwardness. He folded his napkin twice before speaking.

"Do we pray?" he asked.

"We remember," Helen answered.

Lev sat last.

He looked different in daylight—less ghost, more echo. He wore the same coat but had removed the scarf. His hair was damp from snowmelt, and his hands were scrubbed clean, the knuckles chapped.

He stared at the food, brow furrowed.

"It smells like my grandmother's kitchen," he said. "But I never knew where it came from."

Helen handed him the bowl of potatoes. "Now you do."

The first minutes were stiff. Awkward.

Forks clinked. Throats cleared.

Then Avi muttered, "This bread still has beets in it?"

"Yes," Leah replied.

"Jesus," he said. "I hated that as a kid."

Helen rolled her eyes. "And yet you always ate three slices."

Avi smirked. "I was trying to be polite."

"Since when?"

They laughed—short, surprised. It wasn't ease. But it was **motion**.

Leah passed the chicken. Saul raised his glass—silent this time, just a nod. Elena whispered to Jacob, "Who was the man in that fishing photo again?"

Lev leaned over and answered.

And just like that, **conversation returned**.

Not as performance.

But as **reclamation**.

They spoke of Yusuf—not just the man who folded letters into his coat or built a new identity from the ashes of another, but the father who fixed a door hinge with spit and thread, who stared at the TV but never laughed at sitcoms, who only ever danced once—drunk, barefoot, holding Anya's hand in the middle of the living room while war raged overseas.

They spoke of Anya—not just the saint in memory, but the woman who could be sharp, who once slapped Helen with a dish towel for mouthing off, who cried while chopping onions because they reminded her of home.

They spoke of Rosa, of Saul's wife, of children not born, of traditions never claimed.

They spoke of **their family**, not as a tree, but as a tangled vine—part wild, part cultivated, all of it reaching for the same patch of light.

And then came the moment no one planned.

Lev unfolded the last photo he'd brought. One no one had seen before.

It was Yusuf. **Smiling.**

Not the thin, formal kind. But laughing. Head thrown back. Shirt open at the collar.

He was standing in a field beside Kerem—Lev's grandfather. Arms around each other. Dirt on their shoes. Joy on their faces.

"They were happy, once," Lev whispered.

No one spoke for a long time.

Then Leah stood.

She tapped her glass. Not loudly. Not commanding.

"I have something," she said. "Something Anya once said."

They turned to her. Waited.

"She said every family is a table. And every secret is a missing chair. But if you leave it empty, it becomes a ghost. If you name it, it becomes a place."

She pointed to the three empty chairs.

"This is our naming."

And then—finally—**they ate.**

With full mouths and open hearts.

They passed food without counting servings. They told stories without trimming the pain. They cursed. They laughed. Helen cried into her napkin and didn't apologize.

Avi reached across the table and touched Lev's arm.

"I'm glad you came," he said.

Lev nodded. "So am I."

That evening, as the table was cleared, Leah wrapped the remaining bread in wax paper and tucked it into the freezer.

"Why freeze it?" Elena asked.

"For later," Leah said.

"For who?"

And Leah smiled.

"For whoever's next."

ELM STREET – DECEMBER 2005

Elm Street – December 2005

It arrived not with ceremony, but in a plain envelope, shipped from a municipal archive in Vienna, forwarded twice by mailroom clerks who had no idea what they were carrying. Leah found it tucked in a cardboard parcel between photocopies of census pages and shipping records.

She nearly missed it.

The return address was faded. The seal yellowed. Inside, wrapped in protective film, was a letter penned in longhand—familiar, but formal. On the envelope, in Yusuf's script, was a single name:

Leah.

No date. No postmark. Just the weight of it, still sealed after decades.

She sat at the old table on Elm Street, snow pressing quietly against the windowpanes, as if the world itself held its breath.

She opened it with the same care she'd once used to unwrap her grandmother's delicate china. Inside: thin paper folded into precise thirds, and a scent she couldn't place—dust, ink, and something like dried mint.

The words began plainly, without greeting.
To the one I could not burden while I lived—
And just like that, it began to unravel her.

There are names that save us, and names we hide behind.

I have lived as Yusuf Halem for most of my life, but that was not the name I was given. It was one I took—out of fear, yes, but also love.

When I left home, I left behind more than my country. I left a brother. A name. A truth that could not follow me across the sea. I was told that survival here demanded cleanliness—of record, of language, of story. And so I chose a new self.

Kerem was not my brother by blood. He was something more dangerous than that: my other half, my memory. He stayed behind so I could go. And when he asked to come years later, I gave him the only thing I could—my name.

He entered this country as my brother. A paper son. A legal fiction that kept him alive, and made me a liar.

Leah paused, swallowing.

The room seemed darker now. Or maybe the truth had drawn something old out of the walls.

She kept reading.

Anya never knew. Not all of it. She had her suspicions—she always did—but she let me keep my silences because she knew how much they cost me.

There were things we never said to each other. Out of mercy. Out of fear. And that mercy became a wall, and the wall became a room where I lived alone.

I burned the old letters because they reminded me of what I chose to forget. I buried the truth in scraps and half-told stories because I believed it would hurt less that way.

I was wrong.

To live is to choose which ghosts you carry and which you leave behind. I carried mine in silence, and in doing so, I passed their weight to you.

She paused again. Her hand trembled as she reached for her tea, but it had gone cold.

Her eyes scanned the lines again, now blurred.

I want you to know that everything I built was real. The love. The bread. The quiet nights. You were the truest part of my life. Even if I gave you a father who was built, in part, from fiction.

I loved you with a name I chose. But my love was not a lie.

If this letter finds you, then perhaps the silence has finally broken. Perhaps you are ready to know me—not just as your father, but as the frightened boy I once was. The man I had to become. The brother I lost.

I do not seek forgiveness. Only understanding.

Tell them, when the time is right.

Tell them what survival looks like.

Tell them love is not always honest—but it is always real.

Tell them I did not forget.

I simply could not say it aloud.

—**Yusuf**

Leah let the letter fall into her lap.

Not out of carelessness—but because she could no longer hold the weight of it in her hands. Her breath shuddered. A sound broke in her throat, something between a sob and a laugh. She felt no anger. No relief. Only something more complicated—a mourning for the man she thought she fully knew, and the one she now realized had been trying, desperately, to reach her across time.

She looked out the window. Snow still fell. Light, then heavier.

Behind her, on the mantle, sat the silver locket that once belonged to Anya—closed tight, never opened. She stood, crossed the room, and opened it for the first time in years.

Inside was the photo of a boy in a scarf—Anya's brother, left behind.

Now, beside Yusuf's letter, Leah placed it on the table.

Two pieces of history, silent and side by side.

That night, she walked through the house, one last time, touching doorknobs, tracing wallpaper, folding the edges of her family's story into corners and closets.

Tomorrow, she would share the letter.

Tomorrow, the table would be set one final time.

But tonight, she wept—not only for what had been hidden, but for what had endured.

And as the candle burned low beside her, Leah whispered to no one:

"I know now. And I still love you."

ELM STREET – NOVEMBER 2006

The house stood on the edge of memory and winter. Its windows, like tired eyes, looked out across a leaf-littered lawn, pale with frost. There were fewer curtains now. No rugs. Bare walls where photographs once lived. The wallpaper had started to curl at the seams.

But the table remained.

Not Anya's table, but the one that had replaced it when Helen bought the house after her second divorce—solid oak, water-stained, uneven in the legs. It had held laughter, arguments, secrets. Now, it would hold **everything one last time.**

They gathered slowly, uncertainly.

It had been nearly a year since the last Thanksgiving—the one fractured by snow, confession, and a letter that burned with truth. Since then, Leah had traveled. Helen had recovered, though her speech still slurred when she was tired. Sarah had returned to college with a new major—history—and a quiet reverence for the lives that came before her.

And the house, after much debate, had been marked for sale. A cousin was handling the listing. The deal would close by Christmas. This Thanksgiving would be the last.

Helen was the first to arrive, as she always was.

She brought the green beans again—still too soft, still doused in salt and bacon fat. Leah took them with a smile and said nothing. The ritual mattered more than the seasoning.

Jacob came with Elena and their daughter, carrying a casserole dish wrapped in foil and a bottle of wine with a handwritten tag: *From the old country (or close enough)*.

Avi brought stuffing and peace offerings—he had written each guest a small card, tucked discreetly under their plate. "No speeches," he promised. "Just gratitude. And maybe a few things I never said out loud."

Lev came last, carrying a photo album and an envelope. He didn't say what was inside, only that it had come from Vienna—**again.**

And Leah... Leah stood in the doorway, apron on, hair tied back with a ribbon from Anya's old sewing box. She had been cooking since sunrise.

The table filled, course by course, flavor by flavor.

There was turkey, yes, but also lentils spiced with cumin. Dill bread, its crust golden. Roasted beets that bled red into the mashed potatoes. Pickled onions. Hard-boiled eggs. Black tea steeped with mint and sugar, just as Anya used to brew it when money was tight and warmth was needed.

And at the center, lit by two candles: a single plate with a slice of beet bread and a sprig of rosemary.

The plate was not meant to be eaten.

It was meant to be remembered.

Before they sat, Leah spoke—quiet, steady.

"This table held our beginnings and our endings. It has held secrets. Arguments. Love. And now, it holds all of us—what we've kept, what we've lost, and what we're still learning to forgive."

She gestured toward the empty chair beside the plate.

"This is for Yusuf. For Anya. For Kerem. For all the names we didn't know to ask about. This is for the people who gave us the feast—even when they couldn't sit at the table."

There was no applause. Just stillness. Then, one by one, they took their seats.

They ate. Slowly. Reverently. The clink of forks was a kind of prayer.

Stories rose between bites—ones that had never been told aloud.

Helen shared a memory of Anya humming to herself while kneading bread, whispering what she called "seed songs." Songs Leah had thought were lullabies. "They were spells," Helen said. "She believed food needed blessing before it became a meal."

Jacob recounted the day Yusuf taught him how to tie a tie—not by demonstration, but by having him do it wrong six times until the knot held. "He said it would stay better if I learned through failure."

Even Saul spoke. Just once. Quietly.

"He loved you all. He just didn't know how to say it."

No one asked who he meant. They all knew.

After dessert—Elena's clove cake and Sarah's experimental apple tart—they cleared the dishes together, not as a chore but as ritual.

They scrubbed pans and dried plates and wrapped leftovers with the kind of care usually reserved for heirlooms.

And then, before anyone could drift away too quickly, Leah returned to the table with one last thing:

A cloth-bound journal. Leather. Worn. Embossed on the front:

Family, Remembered

Inside: recipes, stories, photos, maps. Margins filled with scribbles. Notes in three languages.

She passed a copy to each person.

"It's not finished," she said. "It never will be."

They opened them like scripture.

As the night wound down, and coats were gathered, and final hugs given, Leah stood alone in the dining room. The candles had melted to pools of wax. The air was thick with cinnamon, smoke, and something she could not name.

She looked at the empty plate again. The bread untouched.

And for a moment—just a moment—she swore she heard Anya's voice.

"Feed them with truth. And they'll come back."

Outside, the first snow of the season had begun to fall.

ELM STREET – NOVEMBER 2006, LATE EVENING

The meal had ended. The candles were low, stuttering shadows across the table like closing eyelids. And yet no one quite wanted to leave.

They lingered, as people do when something final has occurred, but the body hasn't caught up to the soul. The food was gone, the words spent. But something sacred hung in the air still — a hush not of grief, but of deep recognition.

The kind that follows truth.

Leah rose first.

She began to gather plates, stacking them two at a time, careful not to scrape the remaining sauces — remnants, as Anya would've said, "for the ancestors."

Helen followed, slower, one hand steadying her hip as she collected spoons and crumpled napkins. Her stroke had left her body a little crooked, her words not always immediate, but the rhythm of her movements now was memory-driven. A woman who had cleared tables after every kind of silence — rage, laughter, mourning.

The others followed suit. No one was asked. No one assigned.

Even Avi, who had once left family dinners early just to avoid the dishes, rolled up his sleeves and began to rinse.

The kitchen filled with quiet clinking — warm water running, a pan soaking, spoons nested into the sink like sleeping birds. Jacob dried. Elena packed up leftovers with the tender precision of someone wrapping history.

Sarah, the youngest adult in the room, stood by the stove watching the last curls of steam rise from a teacup someone had forgotten.

Then she said it, softly, like asking a favor of the past:

"Can someone show me how to make the bread?"

The room stilled.

Not from shock — but from the weight of that simple request.

Leah turned, dish towel in hand. "The beet-dill?"

Sarah nodded. "The one from the story. From Anya."

Leah didn't answer right away. She just nodded — once, firmly — and pulled open the drawer near the sink, removing a stained index card in Anya's handwriting.

"It's not exact," she said. "She measured with her hands. A palm of flour. A thumb of salt."

"That's okay," Sarah replied. "I think I'd rather measure it that way too."

They cleaned for another hour, but it felt like minutes.

And in that time, something began to shift.

They weren't just wiping countertops. They were sealing something closed. With every dish washed, with every chair pushed back under the table, the ghosts in the room softened. Not vanished — never that — but calmed, soothed by the rhythm of hands working side by side.

The house, too, seemed to exhale. Floorboards creaked not in protest, but as if loosening after decades of holding too much.

When they were done, the kitchen gleamed. Not perfectly. But lovingly.

Leah walked from room to room, turning off lights.

The dining room. The hallway. The parlor where Yusuf once fell asleep with Helen's baby photo resting on his chest.

Each click of a switch was an amen.

Back in the kitchen, Sarah stood holding the recipe card.

"I want to make it next year," she said. "Even if it's just for me."

Leah met her gaze, eyes shining.

"That's how it starts."

Sarah looked around — at her elders, the cabinets, the dust motes that danced in the lamplight — and whispered:

"We should keep something from here. Not just stuff. Something that breathes."

Leah smiled. "We will."

That night, long after the others left, Leah sat alone in the kitchen.

The scent of dill still lingered in the air. The bread pan had been scrubbed clean, but the spirit of it remained. She set the recipe card beside her journal and opened a blank page.

She titled it:

For the Ones Who Stayed

Then, beneath that:

Beet-Dill Bread — As Remembered

She began to write.

TWO WEEKS LATER – LEAH'S APARTMENT, BROOKLYN

It started with bread.

Or maybe it started long before that—with stories folded into pastry crusts, with dill sewn into the windowsill light of a tenement, with Anya whispering to dough as if it could carry memory.

Leah's kitchen was small—narrow, with cracked tile and a stubborn oven—but it felt like the right place to begin. The house on Elm Street was gone now. Sold. Emptied. Stripped of furniture, yes, but never of meaning. She had taken very little from it—a chipped teacup, a photograph of Yusuf squinting in sunlight, and the old wooden recipe box, still lined with yellowed index cards and notes written in three languages.

She laid it all out on the table. Each card, each scribbled grocery list, each stained napkin with instructions written hastily in a grandmother's hand.

Some were recipes. Others were more like spells.

"Steep the chamomile until it smells like home."

"Cut the beets while thinking of someone you love."

Leah smiled as she read them, her fingers trembling only slightly as she smoothed the paper with her palm.

She began to write.

Not just ingredients, but **context**.

She titled each entry with a name and a moment.

Beet-Dill Bread (Anya, Thanksgiving 1914)

"Made from bruised roots, scraps, and hope. Best eaten in silence, with someone who makes you feel safe."

Cabbage Soup with Stolen Salt (Tenement, Winter 1915)

"Boiled until the windows fog. Stir only clockwise, to keep the past from returning."

She included variations, annotations, and fragments of family lore.

"Yusuf preferred mint over lemon in the tea—but only after 1942."

"Helen always added too much pepper. No one told her."

She added voices where she could remember them. Footnotes of memory. Recipes that weren't just food but **ritual**—acts of survival that became nourishment.

The journal grew thick.

What began as a notebook soon became something else entirely—a quilt made of pages. A family history told through meals.

She added photographs: the bread pan, Yusuf's chipped mug, a grainy snapshot of Helen holding a pie with a burned crust and a triumphant grin.

She left pages blank too.

Not from omission, but from reverence. Spaces for the untold, for what memory hadn't yet revealed, or for the next generation to record.

She titled the book:

The Family Table: Recipes for Those Who Remember

And beneath it, in smaller script:

"Not every ingredient is edible. Some are made of silence. Some are made of fire."

When the first draft was done, she made copies.

Not digital. Not printed at some faceless press. But bound by hand, on thick paper, with thread that reminded her of Anya's old sewing kit.

She mailed them, one by one, to every cousin, every child, every person who had once sat at the table—even those who had left in anger or drifted into silence.

Each copy came with a note:
"This is what we built together. Add to it. Tell me what's missing."

A week later, she received the first reply.

A photo from Sarah, flour on her cheeks, holding up a lopsided beet-dill loaf like a trophy. Beneath it: *"Not perfect. But mine."*

Then came a message from Avi: *"I made the broth. It tastes like when I still believed in things."*

Jacob called and asked if she remembered the pear tart Helen once ruined with salt instead of sugar. He had baked one anyway. "She'd haunt me if I didn't."

Even Lev sent a letter, handwritten, in which he said only:

"I translated the first three recipes into Yiddish. Thought someone should."

In the quiet that followed, Leah sat back and looked at the last empty page.

She didn't know what the next chapter would be—only that it would be written, eventually, around another table, in another kitchen, by someone else with ink-stained hands and a story they weren't yet ready to tell.

But for now, the book was full.

And so was she.

NEW YORK CITY – LATE NOVEMBER, 1917

The chill of late November seeped through the thin walls of the tenement on the Lower East Side. Outside, the streets bustled with the sounds of vendors calling out their wares, children playing, and the distant hum of streetcars. Inside their modest apartment, Anya stood over a small stove, the warmth from the oven offering a respite from the cold. She was preparing a meal, simple yet significant—a roasted chicken, some boiled potatoes, and a loaf of beet-dill bread, its aroma filling the room.

Yusuf entered, his coat dusted with snowflakes, a smile breaking across his face as he inhaled the familiar scents.

"It smells like home," he said, removing his hat and gloves.

Anya turned, wiping her hands on her apron.

"It's our first Thanksgiving here," she replied. "I thought we should mark it, even if it's not our tradition."

They sat at the small table, the flickering candle casting shadows on the walls. As they ate, they spoke of their journey—of the hardships faced, the family left behind, and the hopes they held for the future. Each bite was a testament to their resilience, each word a thread weaving their past into their present.

After the meal, Anya placed a small plate with a slice of bread and a sprig of dill on the windowsill.

"For those who couldn't be with us," she whispered.

Yusuf nodded, understanding the silent tribute.

That night, as they lay in bed, the sounds of the city lulling them to sleep, they felt a sense of belonging—not just to a place, but to each other, and to the new life they were building together.

Decades later, their granddaughter Leah would recreate that meal, drawing strength from the same recipes, the same stories, and the same spirit of gratitude. In doing so, she would honor the legacy of Anya and Yusuf, ensuring that their journey, their love, and their first Thanksgiving would never be forgotten.

BROOKLYN – NOVEMBER 2007

It was the first Thanksgiving not held in the house on Elm Street.

There was no creaking of that old hallway floorboard, no hum of the radiator that always wheezed to life too early, too loud. No Yusuf's chair in the corner. No ghost of Anya passing between stove and table, whispering blessings into bread dough.

But there was a table.

Leah had cleared her apartment of everything not essential and dragged in two mismatched folding tables. A cousin lent her extra chairs. She borrowed tablecloths. The plates didn't match. The forks were thin. But when she stepped back, it looked — almost — like home.

In a way, it was.

This was the first Thanksgiving she would host alone. But not truly alone.

Sarah arrived first, arms full of Tupperware and fire. She had made the beet-dill bread — this time round, it rose just right.

Next came Eli and his partner — both professors now, both surprised to be invited but even more surprised by how easily they slipped into rhythm. Then came two children, their mother gone but her stories intact. Then Jacob's oldest daughter, wearing earrings that had once belonged to Helen.

One by one, they came — some invited formally, others with word passed down like gossip. A few brought children. One brought a photo of her grandmother and placed it beside the pitcher of cider.

No one talked about politics. Not at first. Not out of avoidance, but reverence.

Because this day was not about opinions, but offerings.

The food was imperfect, and that was the point.

The stuffing collapsed in the oven. The sweet potatoes burned along the edge. The cranberry sauce came from a can — but someone shaped it into a flower. Laughter began with the first glass poured. Tension loosened its grip.

As they sat, Leah stood, hands on the back of her chair, eyes soft.

"We used to have a table with ghosts," she said. "Now, we have a table with stories."

There were murmurs of agreement. A few eyes wet.

"We eat to remember. And we keep eating to keep remembering. That's what Anya taught me. What Yusuf taught me. They didn't have much. But they gave everything."

She raised her glass. Others followed.

"To those who fed us, even in silence. To those who found warmth in scraps. To those who came hungry — and stayed."

"To those we didn't know we missed," Sarah whispered.

"To those we make room for," added someone from the end of the table.

A child — maybe seven — reached for another roll.

"Is this the bread with dirt and secrets?" he asked seriously.

Laughter burst from the table.

"That's the one," Leah said. "Taste it slow."

Later, after dishes and storytelling, when the candles had burned down and the guests had gone, Leah sat alone for a moment at the now-empty table.

In front of her sat a small linen-bound book.

The Family Table: Recipes for Those Who Remember

She flipped to the last page.

Blank.

Waiting.

She picked up her pen.

2007 – First Thanksgiving in Brooklyn. A table of strangers, not strangers anymore. The bread rose. So did we.

She capped the pen. Closed the book.

And smiled.

BROOKLYN – NOVEMBER 2007, LATER THAT NIGHT

The dishes had been washed, dried, and stacked.

The chairs had been returned to their borrowed homes.

The laughter, the arguments, the toasts — all had faded into a hush so complete it felt like snowfall without snow.

Leah sat alone in the kitchen, barefoot, the hem of her dress damp from a spilled glass of cider. Her hands still smelled faintly of dill, butter, and yeast. The kind of scent that sticks to memory longer than it does to skin.

The table had been cleared, but she'd left one thing untouched: the small, mismatched candleholder with a single half-burnt taper. It had flickered through the meal, unnoticed by most. But Leah had watched it quietly all evening, the way one watches a thread hold together a fraying seam.

Now she lit it again.

Not out of ritual.

But because something inside her wasn't quite ready for the dark.

She turned off the kitchen light. The flame cast tall shadows on the wall — some familiar, others imagined.

She sat down.

Folded her hands.
And breathed.

In her lap rested the old photo of Anya and Yusuf — taken by accident, snapped in front of a church with borrowed coats and tired smiles. Behind them, the first house they'd ever rented. Leah had found it tucked inside a box of recipe cards, behind a recipe for bread Anya never wrote down but always remembered by heart.

Leah traced the outline of her grandmother's jaw with a fingertip. The edges were blurred. The paper smelled like old spice and starch.

"We remembered," she said softly.

She didn't need a reply.

The room felt full anyway.

Outside, the city churned on: lights blinking across the skyline, a bus braking at the corner, a dog barking two floors down. Inside, all was still.

She whispered the names to herself — all of them. Those who had come. Those who had left. Those who had vanished like mist off the docks.

She said them slowly. Carefully. Like a blessing and a roll call at once.

And then she said one more word.

"Thank you."

Not to any god in particular. Not to fate.

Just... to the ones who tried. The ones who stayed. The ones who stitched a new life from old threads, and passed it down through bread and language and silence and love.

The flame flickered low.

She leaned in, kissed two fingers, and touched them to her heart.

Then she blew it out.

Darkness bloomed gently in the room.

But Leah did not feel alone.

Not anymore.

THE END
(of Book Two — *Final Feast*)
(but never of the table it built)

SOMEWHERE IN THE FUTURE – UNSPECIFIED YEAR

It started with a child.

A girl — maybe eight, maybe ten — with ink under her fingernails and lint on her leggings, sitting cross-legged on the creaky wooden floor of a small community library that smelled of radiator heat and worn spines. A quiet place. A forgotten place.

The book wasn't on the shelf.

Not exactly.

It had been tucked sideways behind a row of donated cookbooks, wedged between *Betty Crocker's 100 Best Casseroles* and *Baking with Joy: A Southern Story in Sweets*. Its spine was linen, fraying along the edge. There was no author's name on the cover. Just a title stamped in fading ink:

The Family Table: Recipes for Those Who Remember

The girl pulled it free and flipped to the first page. The paper was soft — the kind that remembered being handled. Some pages had corners turned down. Others bore faint oil smudges, or children's scribbles, or notes in the margins:

use dill if you have it

never let it rise too long — Anya didn't!

Yusuf hated raisins
She read it like a map.
Not just for ingredients, but for people.

She sat cross-legged under a window, warm light pooling over her like honey, and turned to a page marked with a pressed leaf and a faint pencil sketch of a kitchen window.
First Thanksgiving – 1917
Beet Bread with Dill (Anya's)
No photo. No long story about pilgrims or cranberry sauce. Just a memory written in the plain, aching voice of someone who had *been hungry* and had chosen, in spite of everything, to still give thanks.
The girl read it slowly.
Twice.
By the time she reached the last line —
"We eat to remember. We keep eating to keep remembering."
— she realized her hand was resting over her chest, like she'd seen her grandmother do when remembering someone who was gone.
She didn't know who Anya was.
But she did.
In the way children *know* things they haven't been taught but have always carried.

That night, she slipped the book into her coat and brought it home.
Not stolen — not really. The library hadn't had a scanner for years, and the front desk clerk was asleep in a folding chair.
She laid the book on the kitchen table like a small miracle. Her mother found it while chopping carrots.
"Where did this come from?" she asked.
"It found me," the girl said.
"Don't be poetic. I'm tired."
"I already started the yeast," she added.
Her mother stared, then laughed — surprised, not unkind.

"You even know what yeast is?"
"It's how bread remembers who it's supposed to be."

That night, they made bread.

The dough was messy. The flour got everywhere. They burned the first loaf.

The second one rose.

The kitchen filled with the strange, warm scent of beet and dill — earthy, slightly sweet, old. Her mother sniffed the air and narrowed her eyes.

"Your grandma used to make something like this. Only once a year. Right around the holidays. She never wrote it down."

The girl tore off a piece and chewed thoughtfully.

"Maybe someone else did."

They sat at the table as the bread cooled.

The mother rested her chin in her hand.

"Did your grandmother ever tell you the story behind it?"

"No," said the girl.

"Do you want to know?"

"No," she said again, smiling this time. "I want to taste it first."

Later, when her mother had gone to bed and the house creaked with winter silence, the girl sat at the table again. She turned to the back of the book, where there were a few blank pages — left intentionally.

At the top of the first empty one, she wrote:

Thanksgiving — Today

It was burnt, and weird, and perfect.

We laughed.

We remembered someone we didn't even know we'd forgotten.

We will try again.

Then, in tiny script at the bottom of the page:

To the ones who came hungry — and stayed.

She closed the book.

And somewhere, just past midnight, she lit a single candle — and whispered:
"Thank you."

THE END
(or, more truly — *the table is open again*)

Thank you for joining me on this journey.

If *Final Feast* gave you something to hold onto—a truth, a tear, a thread of healing—I hope you'll take a moment to share your experience with other readers. Your review is more than feedback—it's part of the legacy this family leaves behind.

✎ Reviews on Amazon, Goodreads, or any book platform help others discover the series and mean the world to me as an author.

With all my thanks,

— **Mira Halden**

www.ingramcontent.com/pod-product-compliance
Lightning Source LLC
LaVergne TN
LVHW020430080526
838202LV00055B/5111